For Mom and Dad,
and GN with love
—T. D.

For Ann
—H. J.

VIKING
Published by the Penguin Group
Penguin Putnam Books for Young Readers, 345 Hudson Street, New York, New York 10014, U.S.A.
Penguin Books Ltd, 27 Wrights Lane, London W8 5TZ, England
Penguin Books Australia Ltd, Ringwood, Victoria, Australia
Penguin Books Canada Ltd, 10 Alcorn Avenue, Toronto, Ontario, Canada M4V 3B2
Penguin Books (N.Z.) Ltd, 182-190 Wairau Road, Auckland 10, New Zealand

Penguin Books Ltd, Registered Offices: Harmondsworth, Middlesex, England

First published in 2000 by Viking, a division of Penguin Putnam Books for Young Readers.

1 3 5 7 9 10 8 6 4 2

Text copyright © Teri Daniels, 2000
Illustrations copyright © Harley Jessup, 2000
All rights reserved

LIBRARY OF CONGRESS CATALOGING-IN-PUBLICATION DATA
Daniels, Teri.
Just enough / by Teri Daniels ; [illustrated by Harley Jessup].
p. cm.
Summary: A young boy describes himself as old enough to feed the fish,
bold enough to hold a worm, and sweet enough to give a gift.
ISBN 0-670-88873-7 (hardcover)
[1. Self-perception—Fiction. 2. Stories in rhyme.] I. Jessup,
Harley, ill. II. Title.
PZ8.3.D233 Ju 2000 [E]—dc21 00-008395

Printed in Hong Kong

Set in Garamond

JUST
enough

by Teri Daniels / pictures by Harley Jessup

VIKING

SMALL

enough to see my shoes,
below the bed,
very red
shoes.

CALM

*enough to keep my seat,
a rest my feet
when I eat,
seat.*

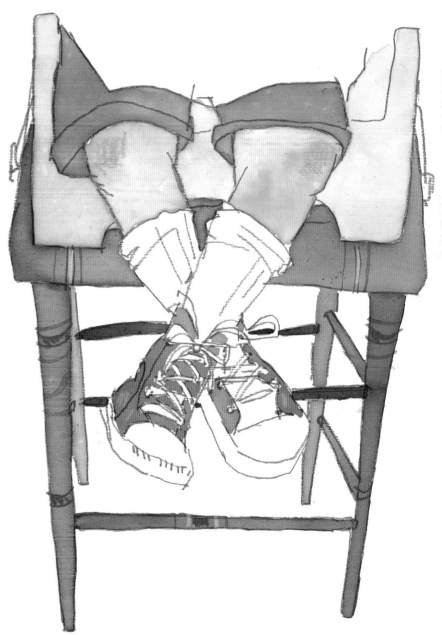

OLD
enough to feed the fish,
the wiggle 'round,
squiggle down
fish.

BIG

enough to build a house,
a stack it tall,
let it fall
house.

STRONG

*enough to pound the dough,
the push it flat
when we pat
dough.*

CLEAN

*enough to wipe a spill,
an apple juice
on the loose
spill.*

SWEET

enough to give a gift,
a pick a bunch
after lunch
gift.

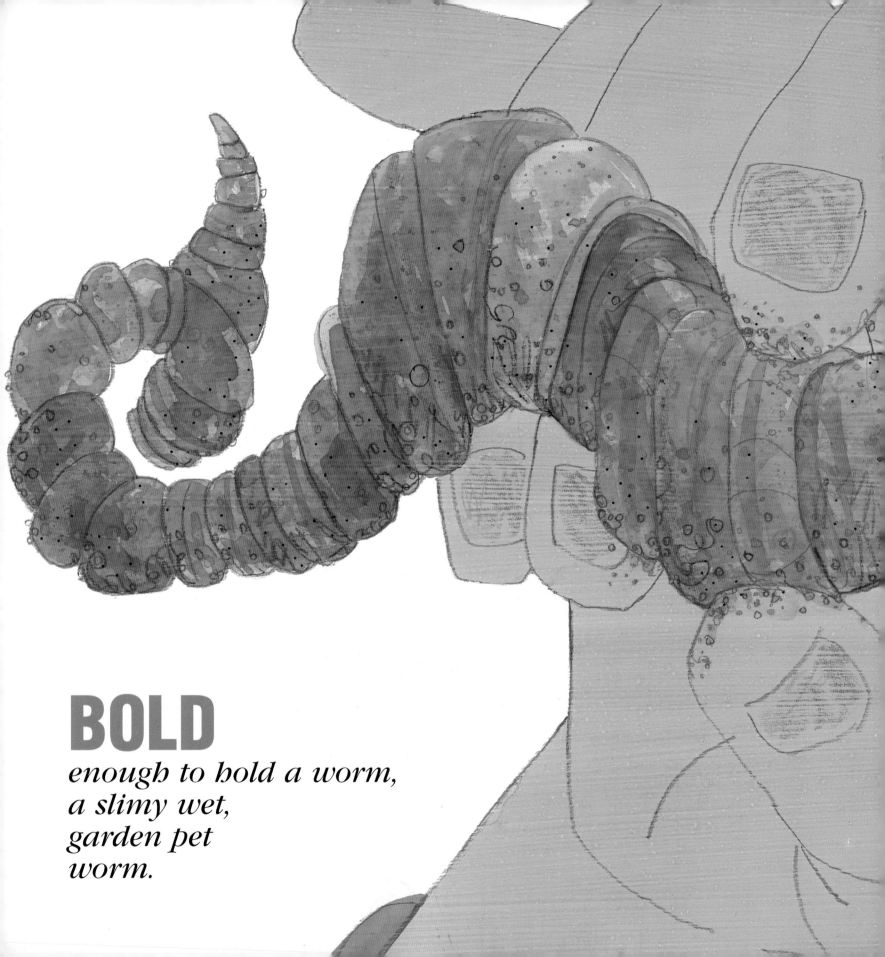

BOLD

*enough to hold a worm,
a slimy wet,
garden pet
worm.*

GLAD

*enough to sing a song,
a shout it out,
dance about
song.*

LOUD

enough to shoo the birds,
the come to look
while we cook
birds.

NEAT
enough to eat my corn,
my take a bite
left to right
corn.

FREE

enough to ride the swing,
the feel the air
blow my hair
swing.

QUICK
enough to catch a bug,
a flicker light
in the night
bug.

TALL
enough to touch the sky,
our twinkle star,
very far
sky.

WILD
enough to splash the bath,
the bubbles pop
at the top
bath.

STILL

enough to fill my cup,
a take a sip,
dribble drip
cup.

SOFT

*enough to pet the cat,
the by my side,
sleepy-eyed
cat.*

NICE

enough to give a kiss,
a peek-a-boo,
I love you
kiss.

BRAVE

enough to say good night,
a pillow puff,
just enough,
feels so right,
tucked in tight …
night.